Do Not Feed
The Zombies

And Other Stories

Justin Johnson

Do Not Feed The Zombies: And Other Stories

Justin Johnson

I greatly appreciate you taking the time to read my work. Please consider leaving a review wherever you bought the book, or telling your friends or blog readers about this book, to help me spread the word.

Thank you for supporting my work.

Justin Johnson

CONTENTS

A SHORT STORY FOR KIDS AGES 9-12

DO NOT FEED THE ZOMBIES

JUSTIN JOHNSON

DO NOT FEED THE ZOMBIES

October 31, 3015

I leaned over and whispered to Aiden, "How long do you think he's been in there?"

Aiden answered without giving it much thought, "It's difficult to tell. Based on the rot and decomposition along the jaw line, I'd say maybe a few months. But don't quote me on that."

I looked hard at the torn skin and exposed bone. There was no way Aiden was right. This one had been in there much longer than a couple of months. In fact, it wouldn't have surprised me if our tour guide let us know that this particular zombie was the first zombie to ever be held in captivity and put on display.

Looking along the edge of the guard rail that separated us from the 'State of the Art' Zombie display at the zoo, I couldn't help but think that there wasn't a whole lot separating us from the flesh eating lot. And that if they somehow managed to get out of the ten foot deep pit they were in, it would be utter terror and devastation for the rest of us.

The part that was most frightening was that the pit was completely open on the top.

No barrier at all.

None.

I raised my hand and asked the tour guide, "How do you know we're safe?"

He took a second, startled that anybody would even dare ask such a question. He hoisted his belt buckle above his overly extended belly and gave the lapels of his coat a quick jerk before answering.

"Son, this here display was designed completely with safety in mind. The pit has been measured precisely and this guard rail is completely reinforced with the strongest steel mesh imaginable. Not to mention the concrete barrier has been poured to triple the required thickness."

He gave a quick snort and nervously touched his hand to his name tag, giving it a quick downward tug before finishing his response. "So you see, it's quite safe."

Everyone nodded, showing their approval at the guide's explanation.

But not me.

I looked over the edge of the enclosure, staring at the collection of zombies that were gathered below. They looked up at me, making eye contact with their cold, blue eyes.

There must've been ten or fifteen of them. One of them jumped up, attempting to climb out of the pit, its finger tips just missing the top of the super thick concrete wall.

I felt a chill go up my spine. The thought of one of them managing to get loose gave me a quick shudder as we moved on with the tour, in the direction of the lions.

"Are you okay?" Aiden asked, sunflower seeds sticking to his lips as he attempted to spit them out on the ground. He spat and sputtered for a few seconds before he realized I was looking at him. "What?" He asked.

"I'm fine."

"You are a lot of things Darren. But fine is not one of them."

He was right. I hated it when he was right.

"Alright, you got me. I'm a little nervous, that's all."

"What's there to be nervous about?" He asked, motioning to the tour guide, who was setting up in front of the lion cage. "He said it's safe. It must be safe, right? I mean, why would he lie about something like that? And why would they let us into the zoo on Halloween night if it wasn't safe to be here?"

These were all good points, I had to admit. He was absolutely right. There's no way they would have let us into the zoo, especially on the creepiest night of the year, if it wasn't completely safe.

Still, I couldn't help but be distracted by the crowd gathered around the zombie display. And then I saw something that made me realize that our tour guide had omitted a very important piece of information. It may not have even been an intentional choice for him not to tell us. But he had definitely forgotten something.

There was a sign.

I hadn't seen it before because there had been a number of kids standing between it and me.   Not to mention how small it was, considering the crucial piece of information it possessed.

It had five words on it.   Nothing more, nothing less.   Five words that would keep everyone safe from harm, if only they could see them all the time.   If they had raised the sign another six feet, it would be clearly visible for all — Do Not Feed The Zombies.

But on this night of Halloween, I saw a boy with a devious look on his face. He had shaggy hair growing out of a brown baseball cap. The hair was in his eyes and he couldn't help bringing his fingers to his face every five seconds to sweep the hair away.

He was slowly unzipping his backpack and rooting around inside. Clearly he was trying to find something, but I couldn't tell what it was. His tongue came out of his mouth, pinched between his two lips and pointed upward. Instead of looking down at his bag, he was looking up into the sky as if trying to imagine what the inside of his backpack looked like, rather than just unzipping the thing a little more and getting what he needed.

Finally, his hand emerged with a large package that appeared to be wrapped in brown paper. There was white string wrapped around it, no doubt to keep the paper in place. I could see little bits of something dripping from the downward pointing corner of it.

The boy took one more glance over the edge of the super reinforced, no nonsense for your safety beam. He grabbed hold of it and gave it a firm pull.

My attention was quickly brought back to the lions, which stood tall in their cages, growling and roaring at our group. The tour guide had made it a point to give us a little show that not every group gets when they come to the zoo during the day. He gave us a wink, like somehow watching a lion make threatening noises behind a cage was somehow a thrill to us. I rolled my eyes and turned my gaze back toward the boy at the zombie pit.

He was now unwrapping the brown papered object behind his backpack. He was crouched down amongst his group and clearly trying to hide the object.

When he'd removed the paper, he reached back into his backpack and took out a pair of rubber gloves. After he'd managed to slide them on, he picked up the object that was lying on the ground. As it turned out, there were actually two objects, both of them were red and dripping.

Steaks?

The boy looked around and as he spotted me, he raised the two steaks slightly and nodded a smile in my direction. And then he walked over to guard rail and heaved both of them into the zombie pit. Before anyone could notice what had been done, the boy removed the rubber gloves, wrapped them in the sheet of brown paper and shoved them quickly into his backpack.

Then he walked over to where his class had gathered.

A loud noise came from the opening in the pit. It sounded like the screeches of wild animals fighting over wild flesh. Next to that, the lions behind the cage couldn't possibly hold our attention.

We, along with a few of the other groups that were taking the Halloween zoo tour, came together at the zombie attraction.

I found myself standing next to our tour guide. As I looked up, I could see the concern on his face as the crowd gathered.

By the time we got there, it had been determined that someone had thrown some sort of food into the pit. Of course, I knew that already. I looked for the boy with the brown hat on, but he was nowhere to be found.

"Are you sure this enclosure is safe?" I asked our tour guide again.

This time he was not quite so sure of himself. He bit his bottom lip, ran his hand through his hair and swallowed hard.

"I sure hope so kid. I've never seen the zombies do anything like this before."

"Seriously? You've never been around them during feeding time before?"

"No," he said pulling a handkerchief from his back pocket and wiping the sweat off his face. "When it's feeding time, we round them up into an enclosure at the bottom of the pit. They're locked in a triple secured steel room while they eat. And they aren't released back into the pit until a sufficient amount of time has passed. This ensures that they don't have the required energy to escape."

"But you told me—"

He waved his hand at me. "I know what I told you. That's park policy. We have to tell everyone that. Do you think if everyone knew the truth about what goes on in this place that they'd come here for a night like this?"

"So you lied to us?"

"I didn't lie, kid. Get off your high horse, why don't ya. I told you what was true at the time. In the state the zombies were in before, they could not have gotten out."

"So are you saying that they might be able to get out now?" I looked around at the growing crowd, wondering what the implications of such a thing happening might be.

I didn't have to think long.

Two zombies jumped onto the wall of concrete and were now positioned just a few feet front he guard rail. They were walking slowly toward us.

Whether the whole group was in shock, or whether they were just trying to get a good look at a zombie close up, I'll never know, but it took until the zombies were climbing the guard rail for anyone to even move.

There was screaming and running and hiding like I'd never seen before. People scattered in all directions, hiding behind, under, on top of and inside of anything they thought might keep them safe.

I retreated with most of my class to the area behind the lion cages.

Peering around the corner, I could see that two more zombies had joined the fray.

My friend, Aiden, was crouched down next to me.

"Do you remember how many zombies there were down there?" I asked him.

"I didn't count or anything, but I think it looked like maybe ten or so."

"Do you think it's possible that they'll all end up out here?"

"There's no way that'll happen," said an unfamiliar voice. "There was only enough steak for three or four of them to get their fill. The remaining zombies probably didn't even have a chance to smell them."

I turned to see the owner of the voice. He was boy who looked to be about twelve or thirteen. He had a pale face and a buzz cut.

"How do you know?" I asked.

"Promise not tell anyone?"

"Sure," I said. "I won't tell anyone."

He reached behind himself and brought out a backpack. A closer inspection of the bag revealed blood spots around the zipper line.

Also in the zipper line were little strands of shaggy blond hair.

The boy unzipped the bag and revealed a wig, a brown baseball cap and some bloody brown paper wrapped around two rubber gloves.

"You?" I said. "You did this!"

A wry smile formed on his face. "And you said you wouldn't tell."

***

I was in quite the quandary. I didn't know whether or not I should break my promise to the boy and let someone know who was responsible for this outbreak. The rules of promises when your life was in danger were unclear to me. If you don't tell on someone who did something this wrong, then doesn't that somehow make you just as responsible?

Either way it didn't matter. The flesh eaters were approaching now. The good news was there were so many of us and so few of them that they looked confused about who to chase.

They were moving faster than I thought they might. It wasn't like I'd spent a lot of time thinking about how many miles per hour a zombie could run, but in my imagination they'd always been slower.

Our tour guide yelled for everyone to head to the main doors of the zoo.

All of us turned and ran for the zoo entrance. It was chaos beyond chaos. There were a few times I thought I was a goner. I could feel my balance starting to leave me. And the pushes from bodies all trying to move for the same spot made this feel like a losing game of musical chairs.

For a moment, I'd lost track of the zombies. Were they close? Or had we left them in our wake?

As we reached the entrance, it became clear that the hundreds of students and teachers were not going to make it through the double door that allowed smaller groups to pass safely in and out.

I looked back and saw that the zombies were still standing by the lion cages, no doubt sizing up their next meal.

"That's perfect." I looked up and saw that our tour guide was standing next to me. The look of concern was still on his face, but the corners of his mouth were upturned slightly, revealing the beginning of a smile.

"What's perfect?"

"Contingency plan falling into place," he answered. "You see, in the event that there was ever a zombie escape, the plan is to head for the entrance and lock the doors. This would ensure the safety of the zoo's visitors."

He motioned an upturned hand in a semi-circle around us. "As you can see, that part of the plan is taking place right now."

"So what happens next?" I asked, shuffling my feet to try to keep as close to the front of the line as possible.

"I'd rather not say," he said, swallowing hard.

I was disappointed, but knew that it was probably dangerous and top secret.

Looking from the zombies to the doors and back again, measuring the distance between myself and safety was all I could do as I shuffled my feet. The move was slow and steady, but somehow it didn't feel fast enough.

The tour guide was making the same movements with his head. Back and forth, back and forth.

We couldn't have been more than twenty feet from the doors when the zombies decided that they were finished looking at the lions in their cage and began walking toward us.

I felt the hairs on my neck stand up and my mouth was dry as I turned toward the door and tried my hardest not to push the people in front of me. I knew if they fell, we were goners for sure.

It seemed like they were taking two or three steps to my one. I glanced at the ground between us and them. Not much longer, I thought. I looked at the door. Not much longer there either. It was going to be close.

Finally, I could smell them. They were close enough for me to get a big whiff of the rotting flesh and the remnants of the steak that'd been thrown their way.

I wasn't far away from the door, but somehow it felt this was the end. I closed my eyes and felt my body get rigid and tight.

And then something grabbed my arm and began to pull. I resisted at first, thinking that this was not the way I wanted to die. But the tug came harder and harder.

"Come on, kid!" I heard the tour guide say, my feet moving in his direction.

I opened my eyes and saw that his hand was on my arm, tugging me to safety.

When I had crossed the threshold, I fell to the floor and looked up just in time to see the doors slam shut. Another man wearing a zoo uniform came up to the door and locked it.

There were gasps of horror.

"What are you doing? You can't lock the door yet!" The voice belonged to a woman who had rushed through the crowd to plead her case.

Getting to my feet, I walked up the window that looked out into the zoo. And then I gasped.

There was still one student outside. He had a buzz cut and his already pale face was so colorless it was almost transparent. He looked up and his eyes met mine, just before the zombies grabbed the bag that was hanging from his shoulders.

***

"We have to do something," I said to our tour guide. "We can't just leave him out there!"

"I understand that," he said. He reached for his walkie talkie and held it to his mouth. "Begin phase two."

"What's phase two?"

He nodded his head toward the window and said, "Keep watching."

I turned my attention back toward the park. The kid outside had managed to free himself from his backpack and was now sliding back toward the door like a crab.

The zombies were fighting with each other over the backpack. The fight became so fierce that one of them bit a finger off another one. They'd pulled the bag so hard in different directions that it was beginning to fray. And eventually it tore open and the boy's wig and hat, along with the bloody brown paper flew into the air and fell to the ground.

The zombies dropped to their knees and began to ravage the paper.

I had been so distracted by this, that I barely noticed the lions and bear roaming free from their cages. They were walking in the direction of the zombies, making no effort to conceal themselves.

The boy continued to slide slowly toward the locked doors of the zoo.

We all watched in anticipation, wondering what would happen if the zombies were to notice that they were being stalked.

As the boy got closer to the door, the man in the zoo uniform unlocked it.   The clicking sound of the lock was enough to distract the zombies from their analysis of the brown paper.

They looked up, confused.

The boy was pulled to safety and the door was locked once again.

And not a moment too soon. The zombies took off in different directions, as did the animals, scattering and chasing the undead men.

The tour guide put his hand on my chest and guided me away from the window.

"Everybody, step back please," he said, before pushing a button on the wall.

A giant sheet of black steel began to rise from the floor, blocking our view of the park.

I looked up a the tour guide.   My eyes must've looked disappointed.

"It's best you kids not see what's about to happen. You've been through enough already."

I nodded. And though I was curious, I knew he was right.

My class turned and walked toward our busses, conversations sparking slowly before becoming a full fledged fire of excitement.

I walked silently and looked in the direction of the boy who'd started the whole thing.

He was being led, rather forcefully, by his teacher. His head was down and she was silent.

I was glad he was alright and that we would all be leaving the zoo in one piece tonight.

The boy had made me promise not to tell anyone. This came back to me as I stepped onto my bus and sat down.

Staring at the giant welcome sign, I couldn't help but think that sometimes you don't have to say a thing. Sometimes things just work out.

My friend Aiden found me after we'd been on the bus for a few minutes.

"Hey," he said. "Do you know what happened? They said some boy..."

His story continued as I smiled and listened. I just let him go on as the bus pulled away. There was no need to interrupt, or listen too closely.

I saw the whole thing with my own two eyes.

SKEETER SKUNK AND THE GLANDULAR FUNK

Skeeter was hiding behind a large oak tree. It was the perfect tree to hide behind. It was tall and wide and surrounded by many other trees. He was peeking around the edge of the tree, watching his friends. He and the gang were playing hide and seek and he was the only one left to be found. He chuckled to himself, giddy with excitement over the hiding place he'd chosen.

His hiding place was so good that the seeker had asked for the help of all of the other participants to find Skeeter. Skeeter was just getting ready to settle in for a long wait. He laced his fingers behind his head and sat down at the base of the tree.

The calls of his friends gave him the titters.

"Is he over there?" Skeeter recognized the voice of Renee Racoon. She had the best nose of all of his friends. She could find the only piece of beef in a dumpster full of food. And yet, here she was in the middle of the forest, unable to find, arguably, the smelliest of all wild creatures.

"No," said another voice. This one belonged to Morty Mole. Skeeter honestly didn't even know why he was playing.   He was blind for one thing. And for another, he did his best work below the ground.

"Boo!"

The deep, booming voice came as a shock to Skeeter, who in his distraction, had let his guard down and was not prepared to be found quite so soon. He didn't have time to think before his body reacted instinctually and sprayed forth a fine mist of stench.

His mother and father had told him about this before. They said it was a good thing, even if it seemed like a bit of nuisance at first. They told him, "One day it'll save your life."

Skeeter had never experienced the mist before this moment, and now that he looked back on his conversation with his parents, he couldn't help but think that, perhaps, they were just trying to be positive about something very negative.

The cloud enveloped him now, along with Ricky Rabbit, the pesky culprit who'd scared him, and forced him to express his fright in a rather gag worthy way. The two fell to the ground, though they weren't too far away from the ground to begin with, and rolled around covering their faces and coughing.

Renee and Morty kept a safe distance, watching their friends roll around in the most peculiar way.

"Is everything alright over there?" Renee asked.

"Yeah," Morty said, concerned. "You look like you're in pain." He turned to Renee. "Don't they look like they're in pain?" He looked back toward Skeeter and Ricky and squinted.

"You're hardly the best one to be the judge of that now, are you?" Renee quipped. "You're blind as a bat."

"Don't you dare compare me to that insulant creature," Morty replied, holding an angry finger up to what he thought was Renee's face. However, Morty's eyes failed him again. His finger was actually nowhere near Renee's face, but rather was pointed at the back of Renee's head, making the gesture wholly ineffective.

Renee ignored Morty. "I think we should go check on them." But then she stepped forward two paces. Even from this far away, there was a faint smell of hideous that had made its way through the woods. They had to have been at least fifteen trees away, a good twenty feet. There was no way one of Skeeter's or Ricky's farts could have made it that far, could it?

"Do you smell that?" Renee asked Morty, who was still steaming about being compared to a bat.

"I don't know what you're talking about," Morty pouted sourly. "And even if I did, I doubt very much I would...Oh, my goodness gracious my!" Morty was gagging and sputtering through his words, trying not to throw up while he spoke. It took every ounce of control to force his nasal passage to close, so he could speak and breath through his mouth. "I smell it now. Wow, is that strong or what?"

Renee nodded, but Morty didn't see. "I don't dare go any closer," she said. And then she squinted, giving the situation a closer look. Ricky appeared to be wiggling away from Skeeter now, crawling on his belly, his front legs working double time to drag his rear feet behind him, lest he get too far away from the ground and stick his head directly into the cloud of stink.

Skeeter's faint cries could be heard through the trees. "Wait, don't leave me here. I don't know what this is going to do to me. Help!"

"We must go help him," Morty commanded, stepping forward. He had walked four, maybe five feet, when he suddenly turned around and walked back to where he'd been standing. "On second thought, he'll be fine."

Within a few very tense and quiet moments, Ricky had emerged from the cloud and took a spot next to Renee, who was watching Skeeter with a great deal of concern. Granted, it wasn't enough concern to put herself into harm's way, but she was worried. She was so deep in her mind, wondering about whatever could have happened to Skeeter, that she didn't realize how bad Ricky smelled until he spoke and broke her trance.

"What do you think it is?"

"I don't —" She had to cut herself off or she was going to be adding two pounds of bile covered garbage to the mix. She brought her paw up to her mouth and nose, hoping the smell of last night's garbage would help mask the smell that was now soaked into Ricky's fur.

"What's wrong?" Ricky asked, oblivious that he had absorbed the smell from Skeeter's spray.

"You can't smell yourself, can you?"

Ricky stuck his nose deep into his fur and took in a breath. He brought his head up and shook it and then dove down into another part of his body and took another breath, making sure this one was really deep. "I can't smell anything."

Within a few minutes, Renee's nose, as well as Morty's, had adjusted to the scent of the foul mist. And none too soon. For Skeeter, who'd spent a few extra minutes hiding behind one of the trees, ashamed of what he'd done, decided it was time to come out and consult with his friends.

"I'm so sorry about that guys. I don't know what came over me," he said, offering his most sincere apology. He kept his face close to the ground, averting his gaze and avoiding eye contact.

"It's okay," Renee offered, coughing mildly. "Do you know what that was?"

"My parents told me about it a while back," Skeeter said. "They said it happens when something frightens us. All skunks have it, you know, to protect ourselves. I just had no idea how strong it would be, or that I had no control over it."

"You mean you didn't do that on purpose?" Ricky chimed in.

"No. It just slipped out."

The friends stood there for a long while before Renee addressed Skeeter. "You have to go home and talk to your parents about this new found...talent."

With that, Skeeter and all of his friends headed home for dinner with baths on their minds.

***

Skeeter's father was sleeping beneath the porch of an old farm house when his nose was called to attention. It only took him one whiff to realize it was his son coming home for the night.

He looked out through the lattice work and saw his son, who was walking with his tail tucked in tight to his body, his face pointed down toward the grass.

"What's wrong?" He asked. "Didn't you have fun with your friends?"

"I guess," Skeeter said, climbing into the dwelling through a gap between the porch and house. "Is mom home?"

"Not yet, why?"

"I need to talk to her."

"It'll probably be a while," his father said. "Is it something I can help you with?"

Skeeter thought about this for a minute. He was always more comfortable talking with his mother about these things, as most young animals were. But this was serious and he didn't feel like he could wait any longer.

"Promise you won't laugh?"

"Of course I won't laugh," Skeeter's father answered. He already knew what Skeeter was going to ask him about, and though he found it a little funny, years of experience showing him how insignificant a problem skunk spray actually was, he also knew that it was a very tough topic to wrap your head around as a youngster.

Skeeter took a deep breath and got into it. "My friends and I were playing hide and seek this afternoon. We were out in the woods and I had the best hiding spot ever! I thought I'd be able to stay there forever and never get caught. That was until Ricky Rabbit found me..." Skeeter's voice trailed off and his eyes were distant with the memory of the horror that he'd unleashed in the moments following the discovery.

"And?" His father prompted, startling Skeeter almost as much as Ricky had done earlier in the day.

Skeeter brought his eyes back into the dwelling under the porch, hesitant to look at his father, though he knew how important it was. He finally mustered up the courage and brought his eyes up ever so slightly until they were looking directly at his father's. "I sprayed," he said shamefully.

There was silence for a moment or two. Of course, to Skeeter, it felt like forever.

"Didn't you hear me, dad?" Skeeter pressed. "I said, I sprayed. I was so embarrassed and now I'm here telling you about it and I'm embarrassed again."

"It's okay," his father said, trying to reassure Skeeter that he'd done nothing wrong. "It can be difficult to get that gland under control, especially when you're not used to it."

"It was my first spray," Skeeter added.

"Oh," replied his father, slightly surprised. "You'd never sprayed prior to this afternoon? I'd have expected you'd have let one slip before now."

"Never." Skeeter looked out the side of the lattice work of the porch. He could see the woods in the distance and the memory passed back through his head. Craning his neck back over his shoulder, he looked at his father and thought about how different this conversation would have been if only his mother had been home. He wanted to cry. But he would never allow himself to do that in front of his father.

His father hemmed and hawed for a few minutes, sensing the discomfort within his son. And then he said, "So what did you think about it? How did it feel for you?"

"I don't know," Skeeter answered, pulling himself away from the lattice work and coming back into the main area of the under porch. "I was so surprised by it that I guess I didn't even really think about it. I guess, I would say it scared me more than anything. My friends were around, you know...I guess I was mostly embarrassed that they had to see me do that. And when I caught a whiff of it, that was enough to make me want to bury my head in the dirt and die."

"Don't be silly," his father admonished. "You're a skunk not an ostrich. No son of mine is going to be caught dead, or otherwise, sticking his head in the dirt. It's a terrible defense mechanism. One that, no doubt, results in a number of unnecessary ostrich deaths. Think about it, son. A predator is coming after you and the only thing you can think to do is stick your head in the dirt, making it impossible for you to see your attacker, while your body is still as visible as ever.

"If there's one thing I want you to realize, it's that this is a gift we have. Skunks are able to immobilize our enemies without ever having to fight them. All we have to do is identify where the attack is coming from and then turn in that direction, lift our tails slightly, and unload some of the good old glandular funk on 'em. That's it. End of story."

Skeeter thought about what his father was saying for a moment and then asked, "But what happens when you let that 'glandular funk' out on your friends?"

"To be honest with you, I never sprayed my friends. I can't really answer that question," his father said. The look on Skeeter's face changed instantly, and his father could see that he was in danger of losing any of the good will and trust he'd gained. "I suppose the most important thing for you, and any other young skunk who's learning to spray for the first time, is to learn how to control it."

"That's easy for you to say," Skeeter said. "You already know how to control yours. I'm so afraid to play with my friends again. What if they laugh at me? What if I spray them again and they decide not to play with me anymore?"

"Come with me," Skeeter's father said, moving toward the gap between the porch and the old farm house. He took Skeeter out around the edge of the house and back behind the old barn that led to a pasture. There were a few horses grazing. "Bernie, Theodore?"

The horses poked their heads up from their evening snack. "Yeah, Don? What is it?"

Skeeter tried to hide behind his father, knowing that what his father was about to do might cause Skeeter to blush.

"My boy's just learning how to spray," Don said. "I have to ask a huge favor from you guys."

"What's that?"

"I know it's inconvenient and all, but would you mind letting us practice here at the edge of your field?"

"Don, you've got to be nuts," one of the horses said. "That is one of the worst ideas I've ever heard. Do you know what effect that'll have on feeding time?"

"I know," Don said, apologizing for the absurd request. "Listen, I'll make it up to you. Name your price."

The two horses looked at each other and without speaking, nodded before one of them said, "You know those giant salt licks that Farmer Jones has stashed in the barn?"

"I do indeed."

"We would like four of them."

"I can do that," answered Don. "You'll have them before dawn tomorrow."

Bernie and Theodore were satisfied with the terms of the agreement and they took off on a trot to the opposite side of the field and ate no more. Skeeter's father led him through the bottom of the electrified fence.

"The key to controlling your spray is knowing when to spray. You only spray when an enemy comes too close. Dogs, foxes, certain types of birds...those are our enemies. Most other creatures won't hurt you."

Skeeter nodded that he understood.

His father continued. "All you have to do is turn your back to the predator and lift your tail."

Skeeter turned his back toward the empty field and brought his tail up slightly.

"You're going to want to get that tail up a little higher," his father cautioned. "Otherwise, you'll end up spraying yourself." Skeeter lifted his tail higher so it would be out of the spray's way. "Good," his father said. "Now, you just push out your butt like you're pooping."

"Like I'm pooping? Why like I'm pooping?"

"Your spray glands are located inside your butt. To activate them, you have to give them a little push."

"But what if I poop instead of spray?" Skeeter asked.

"Don't worry about that," his father assured him. "Our bodies are very good at distinguishing fear from just having to go to the bathroom. If you're afraid enough, the glands will practically set to work on their own. Now, stop questioning and just give a little push."

Skeeter took a deep breath and focussed his energy on his backside. He gave a little push and felt a little mist escape. And then, feeling a little more comfortable with the process, he gave a tremendous push. This time he felt a very thick stream of spray come from the glands.

"Okay!" his father said.   "I think that's enough for today's lesson.   You want to go a little easy with that stuff if you don't really have to use it. What do you say we head home for now?"

Skeeter nodded and began the short trek home, sliding his body beneath the fence and feeling very proud of himself. As he was walking along the side of the barn, he heard his father shout out to Bernie and Theodore, "I'll make sure I get you an extra salt lick to make up for all the excess spray!"

The horses neighed their approval and the two skunks headed home.

***

The next day, Skeeter met his friends on the edge of the woods for another game of hide and seek. His friends noticed that he had a sense of confidence that hadn't been there the day before.

"You're not going to spray us today are you?" Ricky Rabbit half joked.

"Nope," Skeeter answered quickly. "In fact, I'm confident that I'll only spray when I want to."

"How can you be so sure?" Renee pressed.

Skeeter smiled, "Let's just say I had a very good talk with my dad last night."

The three friends looked at each other. Morty Mole thought he was looking at his friends.

"Morty," called Renee Racoon. "We're over here!"

"Oh, yes. Of course." Morty quickly turned in the direction of Renee's voice, his cheeks flush with embarrassment.

They gave each other a nod, signaling that everything was okay with them. Though, to be perfectly honest, they were very hesitant.

The game had been going on for a good hour or so and Skeeter'd been found ten or twelve times. Each time he was found he managed to keep his glands suppressed and his friends were regaining their trust in him.

"This is going to have to be it for me," Ricky said, slightly out of breath from having hopped so much. "My parents are having friends over tonight and asked me to be home a little early."

"Okay," the others answered.

"Do you have time for just one more round?" Renee Racoon asked. She was always so sad when their games had to end and always pushed for just 'one more round'.

Ricky nodded and agreed to one more round. But just one more.

As the friends scattered in all directions of the forest floor, looking for just the right spot to hide, Skeeter began counting by the old stump they'd designated as 'safe' for the day. When he'd just about finished, his count approaching the grand old number of ten, he heard a scream. He could tell that it was Ricky Rabbit.

What could be wrong? Skeeter thought. He turned and began looking for his friend, but he was too well hidden.

Skeeter took off into the woods, checking behind every tree and beneath every mossy rock. More screams came, all of them belonging to Ricky. Renee and Morty had emerged from their hiding spots and were now as concerned as Skeeter to find their hidden friend.

"If I know Ricky," said Renee, jogging along, "He went as far back as he could possibly go before you stopped counting. He always does that to me."

They ran for a little over eight seconds and found Ricky with his back up against a fallen tree, a fox inches from his face. Ricky had peed on the ground in hopes of fending off the unwanted visitor. But the fox continued to bear down on him, showing his sharp teeth and snarling a deeply scary snarl.

Skeeter snapped into action.   He rushed up to Ricky and the fox and turned his rear toward the fox's face.

"Ricky, run!" he yelled to his friend as he planted his back feet firmly and began to push his glandular funk. Ricky took off and just narrowly missed the two yellowy streams of defense that Skeeter thrust from his behind. The fox turned in confusion to face the tail end of the skunk who was yelling out orders to his dinner for the night.

When it was all over the four friends were out in the clearing that separated the old farmhouse from the woods.

"Did you see his face?" Renee laughed, grabbing her stomach and rolling around in the long grass.

"No," answered Morty Mole. "I didn't see anything. But then again, I rarely do!" And he joined Renee in the grass, rolling and laughing.

"You saved my life," said Ricky. "That fox was going to eat me, you know."

"I know," Skeeter answered. He looked into Ricky's eyes and saw there was still a great deal of fear. The fox had put a scare into the hare, that much was for sure. "It's okay, he's not going to come back."

"How can I ever repay you?" Ricky asked. "I mean, how could I ever pay you back for my life?"

"There's no need to pay me back. I'm your friend. I was happy to help. Now, go home and enjoy your evening with your family."

Skeeter turned and headed toward his home under the front porch of the farm house, with a new story to tell his dad.

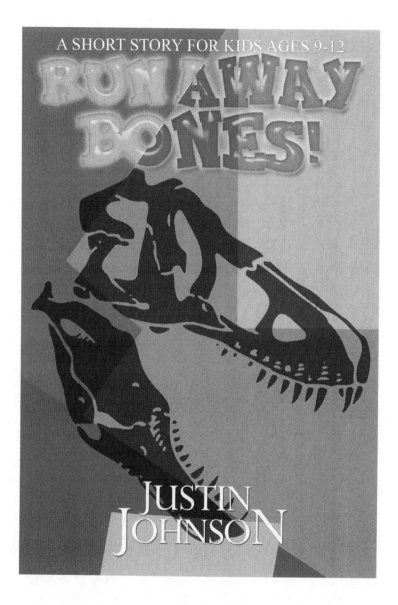

A SHORT STORY FOR KIDS AGES 9-12

RUNAWAY BONES!

JUSTIN JOHNSON

RUN AWAY BONES!

The class huddled around the most intriguing exhibit in the museum, at least in Jayden's mind. He was enamored with dinosaurs, and the idea that someone had gone to such lengths to find the bones of these majestic creatures inspired him. And that they cleaned them up and put them together to form a perfect skeleton brought a smile to his face.

"I still don't see what the big deal is," Gregory whispered in Jayden's ear.

"What do you mean you don't see it? How could you not?" Jayden wasn't really surprised by this. In fact, his friend Greg and him had been having this debate for years.

Greg was always excited about the future and all of the things that men were doing to make their lives better. He thought Jayden was out of touch for looking into the past for answers.

"Are they still alive?" Greg needled.

"No," Jayden responded. "But when they were, they ruled over everything!"

"Shhh!" The tour guide looked at Jayden over small rimmed glasses that sat perched on the tip of a long, narrow nose.

The rest of the kids on the tour turned and looked at Greg and Jayden. They thought it was funny, but had to give the appearance of being upset so as not to attract the attention of their teachers. Jayden looked at Greg and found that he was pointing his thumb in Jayden's direction.

Shaking his head, Jayden took a last look back at the giant T-Rex skeleton that dominated the center of the museum's main entryway. *I've gotta get back to see it one more time* he thought as the tour proceeded.

***

The remainder of the tour was exactly what Jayden thought it would be once they left the dinosaur exhibit — boring. It didn't matter how much he tried, he just could not find paintings of flowers or ancient pieces of pottery exciting.

Greg felt the same way, actually yawning halfway through the tour and, once again, catching the ire of their tour guide, whom Greg had nicknamed 'Specs' by the time everything was said and done.

Just before the group left to board the bus, Jayden took one look back at the gigantic T-Rex statue. He just couldn't help but think that it would be a long time before he saw another sight that amazing, if ever. He gave Greg's shirt sleeve a tug and when Greg turned around, Jayden cocked his head over his shoulder in the direction of the prehistoric beast.

Greg, who could barely keep his eyes open at this point, the thought of lunch the only thing keeping him upright, shrugged his shoulders and followed Jayden, as though he didn't have enough energy to resist.

They walked over to the purple velvet rope that enclosed the mammoth work of art.   Jayden put his hands on the rope, wishing he could climb under it, or over it for that matter, and get a closer look.   He heard a quick cough and looked to his right.

The tour guide was walking toward them now, an angry look in his eyes. Jayden noticed that over the tour guide's shoulder, three busses were pulling out of the parking lot and heading toward the highway.

Swallowing hard, Jayden braced himself for what was coming next.   He and Greg had missed the bus and it was all Jayden's fault.   His teachers would be mad at him, the museum guide was mad at him, Greg would be mad at him and the rest of his classmates would be mad at him, too. Especially when they realized that having to go back and get the two boys would take a considerable chunk of their lunch break.

Jayden closed his eyes, expecting to feel, or at the very least, hear something come his way from 'Specs'. He had the strangest thought as he waited for the very angry man to let him have it.   It wasn't a bad thought, necessarily. But it wasn't the best thought in the world, either.

It was the simple thought that it would be really neat if the T-Rex came to life and saved him from certain punishment and embarrassment.

As he braced himself for the sort of tongue lashing that would accompany such a careless decision, he closed his eyes and waited...and waited...and waited.

Seemingly, nothing had happened.

But when Jayden opened his eyes to look at the tour guide, he didn't see anger on the man's face. He saw fear. The man was looking at something very tall and mouthed the word 'run' to Jayden before turning and running out the front doors of the museum as a full size T-Rex Statue was freeing itself from the rocks it'd been bolted to and took chase.

***

It took Greg a moment to snap out of his stupor. And when he did snap out of it, it wasn't because he'd seen the giant skeleton break free of its moorings, but rather the scream he'd heard form the tour guide he'd named 'Specs'.

"Did you hear that?" he chucked, elbowing Jayden playfully in the ribs.

Jayden didn't move, though he had heard the scream.   He was frozen in fright as he watched the most amazing thing he'd ever seen crash through the front doors of the museum and into the parking lot.

When the skeleton was far enough away from the building, the tour guide emerged from his hiding spot, along the outside wall of the building, and surveyed the damage.

He then brought his eyes toward Jayden and said, "Will you look at what you've done?!   I hope you're happy Mr.

Everything Else In This Museum Is Boring! Look at what you've done!"

"Me?" Jayden asked, pointing to himself. He couldn't believe he was somehow being blamed for a 65 million year old set of bones deciding to come to life and take off. "I didn't do anything!"

"Oh, but you did," said Specs. "You thought to yourself that this would be a great thing. That somehow setting a monstrous wonder of the prehistoric world would somehow be all hunky dory."

"Excuse me," Jayden said, eyes squinted, head cocked to one side. "You think I had something to do with this? You think that just by me thinking this could happen, it happened?"

"Mmm hmm," Specs nodded his head.

"Well if that's the case, why can't I get Carly Granger to go out with me? And how come I didn't do so hot on my math test last week? And why am I still here in this museum with you? If it was that easy for me to just think about what I wanted and have it come true, then why doesn't it work all the time?"

Specs turned toward the door of the museum, which was now just a bunch of shattered glass in the shape of a dinosaur skeleton. "I don't know why it doesn't work all the time, young man. But I do know one thing: It worked this time."

***

At this point, Specs decided that the authorities needed to be notified. Greg and Jayden followed as Specs led them through the main area of the museum and into a locked room. There was a desk in one corner, a few filing cabinets and a table that had what looked to be future museum exhibits on it.

"Don't touch anything," Specs said as he picked up the phone and dialed 9-1-1.

Greg folded his arms in front of his body. Jayden allowed his to hang and took his eyes away from the museum's 'On Deck' table. The sweat was rolling down Specs' forehead. He removed a handkerchief from his pocket and dabbed it lightly. This accomplished very little as the beads that were removed quickly formed again, larger and more abundant than before.

"Hello," Specs finally said into the receiver of the phone. "This is Donald James Willis of the Museum of Natural Treasures. We have an asset out of containment."

Jayden found it hard not to laugh at the thought of the call operator on the other end of the line.

"No, I am not kidding!" Specs said, holding the phone away from his face and looking at it contemptuously. He put the phone back to his ear and said, "When you are finished laughing, I would be happy to report the problem so you can put some men on it. I assure you, this is a serious matter."

It took a few minutes for the man on the other end of the phone to settle down and allow Specs to tell him what was wrong. And when Specs finally did let him know what the problem was, the man snapped into action.

Within a matter of minutes there were five patrol cars skidding into the museum parking lot. The men dressed in blue walked up to the door of the museum, hands on their holsters, and glanced up at the giant dinosaur shaped outline in the glass.

"Who's in charge here?" Asked the Police Chief. He was a large man with a barrel chest. He reached for a small notepad in his front pocket and flipped a few pages. Putting his pen to the paper, he noticed Specs was stepping forward, ready to answer. "And you are..."

"Donald James Willis," Specs said, reaching his hand out for a shake.

"I'm Chief Dennings," answered the Chief, keeping his hands on his notebook and pen. "I can see there's clearly been a great deal of damage here. What did you say caused it, again?"

Specs cleared his throat and blushed as he said, "The T-Rex skeleton." He turned to look at Jayden. "That boy, right there, wished it and it happened." The second the final syllable of his sentence exited his mouth, he wanted it back. As ridiculous as it had sounded in Specs' mind, it sounded a hundred times crazier out in the open with the entire trained police force looking on.

"Right," nodded Dennings sarcastically. "Fredricks, did you hear that? This guy says the boy here wished the T-Rex to life." He chuckled a little as a thin man with a pale complexion and thinning hair walked up next to him. "Can you believe such thing?" The Chief continued. "I mean, Fredricks, in all your life would you ever think it possible for a little kid like this to just wish a giant statue to life?"

Fredricks smirked into his own notepad. "No sir, it doesn't seem like it would even be possible."

The Chief's smile left his face and was replaced by a very serious, no nonsense look. "Now listen here buddy," he said, pointing a finger into Specs' chest. "You tell me right now what happened down here for real, or you're going to go for a ride down to the precinct. If you did something, just come clean. Do you know how small it looks for a grown man to blame their problems on a child."

Specs turned back toward the museum entrance and pointed up. "So if I tell you that the T-Rex statue just lifted itself off its base and took off through the door, then somehow that's more believable than me telling you this kid wished it to happen?"

"Are you telling me that the statue just got up and moved on its own?" The Chief followed up.

"Is it more believable for you when I put it that way?"

The Chief looked around and ran his thick fingers through his dark brown hair. "I don't really know if it's more believable or less believable. But at least you're not blaming your problems on some kid. Even if it was his fault."

Specs shook his head. "Fine. The statue just walked right through the front door...and window for that matter. It walked right across the parking lot and took off down the highway. Now, what are we going to do about it?"

"That's a great question," answered Dennings. "I honestly don't know what we're going to do here. I suppose we'll probably just get into our cars, turn on the lights and sirens and drive down that stretch of highway in hopes of finding it."

Jayden, who'd been silent until now, spoke up. "That sounds cool! Can my friend and I come with you?"

"Normally, I'd say no," replied Dennings. "But the way things have gone today, I really don't have any great reasons why you couldn't come with us."

"Cool!"

"Yeah...cool," said Greg as he looked at Jayden, an untrusting look in his eyes.

***

They were racing down the highway, weaving in and out of mid morning traffic.

Chief Dennings appeared aggravated by the whole thing, like Jayden, Greg and Specs had interrupted something with a higher priority level. His fingers gripped the wheel tight, working back and forth as if trying to wring the life from it. Big gusts of breath kept bursting through the man's lips, followed by the need to roll his head around his neck in varying directions.

The morning sun wasn't quite high enough for Dennings to forgo using the driver's side visor.

Jayden and Greg were in the back seat. Specs had opted to stay back at the museum in case there was another group of kids who showed up to take a tour. Jayden knew this was just a cover for Specs being embarrassed that the T-Rex statue had escaped on his watch, and the fear of what might happen when they eventually caught up to it.

There was a wall of plexiglass between Chief Dennings and the two boys, giving the police chief some much needed silence while he sorted things out.

Jayden crouched down low in his seat and took a look out through the windshield. From this vantage point he could just see the top of the T-Rex bobbing up and down with every step the massive structure took. He looked at Greg, who was slouched down low in the seat, staring out the car door's window. Jayden nudged Greg with his elbow.

"Are you just going to stare out the side of the car and do nothing? Don't you even have the faintest idea how cool this is?"

"It's not cool," Greg said "You set a million year old piece of history in motion. Sent it right down the highway, looking to do God knows what. You've tied up the entirety of the police force for the morning. Hopefully, they don't have any real crimes that need solving while they're out here on this wild Rex chase."

Jayden wasn't sure if he should correct Greg's estimate of the age of the dinosaur and let him know that those bones were well over 60 million years old. He leaned forward in his seat and noticed how tight Greg's lips were pursed. Not to mention the grinding jaw line.

"Hey, look," Jayden said, "It wasn't like I knew that I was going to set the thing in motion. I was just having a simple thought at the wrong time. In fact, it probably wasn't even my thought that did it."

Greg turned to Jayden and measured him with his eyes. "You're probably right. Sometimes things just happen," he said sarcastically. "Just last week, my house grew legs and walked right out of town. It was really hard to find it after school that day. I eventually hunted it down — "

Jayden put up his hand. "Alright. I get it."

Both boys, feeling angry and confused, set their gazes out the side windows of the police cruiser. Jayden couldn't help but wonder if Greg was right somehow. Had he set this whole thing in motion? And if he had, then would he be able to stop it in its tracks?

Time would tell. But for now, he was stuck here in the awkward silence of the back seat of a police car, heading down the highway at top speed.

***

The T-Rex skeleton eventually veered off the highway and ran itself onto a dead end street. It stood there perplexed for a moment as it tried to figure out which direction to go. It looked from house to house while the police cruisers, four in all, took their places around the mouth of the cul-de-sac.

Looking back toward the cars, the skeleton cocked its head quizzically as the police officers threw open their doors and drew their weapons.

While Police Chief Dennings was conferring with his second in command about how to deal with this particular perpetrator, Jayden took off running in the direction of the run away bones.

His friend Greg tried to grab his sleeve, but Jayden jerked his arm away and said, "You're right Greg. I got us into this, I'm going to get us out of it."

The police officers saw Jayden running in the direction of the bony beast and called out for him to get back behind the cars. But there was no use. Jayden had made up his mind to make things right.

As he approached the dinosaur remains he could feel his mouth go dry. He hadn't thought about what he was going to do. He was winging it.

The skeleton looked down at the boy. The police officers raised their guns, pointing them fifteen feet above the head of the boy and directly at the nose of the Rex.

When the T-Rex skeleton fell to the ground harmlessly, it came as a shock to all involved. Everybody that is except Jayden. He walked back to the officers, who had put their guns back into their holsters.

"What did you do?" Dennings asked.

"I used my mind to get him to stop, just like I did back in the museum to get him going in the first place."

"I don't get it kid. That thing was towering over you just a moment ago and then...poof. Out of nowhere it just falls to the ground in a pile of bones?"

"I know," Jayden said. "It's weird isn't it? I didn't think it would work either, but it was worth a try."

"I guess sometimes you just have a connection to something," Dennings commented as he scratched his head.

Jayden thought about this for a few moments and realized that sometimes there's no rhyme or reason for the connections we have with something. Sometimes it's just there. And for Jayden, the connection he had to the past treasures of the prehistoric world were strong. He couldn't explain it to anybody. He couldn't even really explain it to himself. But it was there, and he loved it.

A BOOK FOR KIDS AGES 9-12

the
CARD

JUSTIN
JOHNSON

THE CARD

THE STREET SHREDDER

I was standing at the back of Berkman's store, staring at it! There, high on the wall, begging me to take it home, just out of reach.   All the kids were talking about it, and I couldn't even watch a show without hearing how awesome it was.

What was IT?   Only the best skateboard in the entire world.   The

Street Shredder, Model 2.0, to be more specific. It was shiny and red, with a fire breathing dragon on the smooth side. Plus, it had the coolest neon green wheels.

I must've stood in that same spot, looking up at the *Street Shredder* for hours. I imagined myself flying down the road, the wind whipping against my face as I went faster and faster. The kids in the school yard would all stop what they were doing to look at me as I put my back foot down and came to a super dramatic skidding halt. I would take the opportunity to land a cool jump with a 360 degree turn. And I would kick down on the back of the board and flip it up into my hands and walk victorious into school with the sound of everyone's applause ringing in my ears!

"Hey kid!" I was brought back to reality by the sound of a gruff voice behind me. I turned to see the store manager, a man with a bushy mustache and brown framed glasses. He was walking toward me, a set of keys jingling against his black trousers. "We're getting ready to close the store. Are you gonna buy anything? Or are you just looking?"

And that's when my heart plummeted. I looked back at the *Street Shredder*, the fluorescent lights of the store perfectly illuminating the dragon in all her glory. Taking a deep breath and hoping beyond hope that something had changed since I walked into the store, I reached into my pockets and felt around. Alas, my prayers had not been answered.

"I guess I'm just looking," I answered sullenly.

"I hate to do this, but I have to ask you to leave." He reached for a small walkie talkie that was affixed to the pocket of his shirt. "Larry, don't lock the doors yet. We have one kid in toys on his way up."

"Roger that, boss," came a crackled voice through the speaker.

I shuffled down the aisles, head down past rows of toilet paper and cat food. As I reached the front door, Larry was standing there, hair messed up from gathering carts in the wind. He shot me a grin through his unshaven face and reached for the walkie talkie on his orange vest. "Is he the last one, boss?"

"Yeah."

Larry turned back to me and said, "Have a nice night, kiddo!"

I gave him a half wave and took one last glance at the back wall of the store. Even from this far away, the *Street Shredder* could be seen in its full majesty. It towered above everything else in the store and outshone every last item on the shelf. I knew at that moment that I would own that skateboard. I had no idea how, or where I was going to get the money to pay for it. But I knew it was going to be mine.

THE ASK

On the way home from Berkman's I had made up my mind that I was going to ask my parents.

'How' and 'When' were the two most important questions. If your parents are anything like mine, it does matter how you ask the question, and when you ask the question. For instance, if you come right out with it and blurt, "Mom, Dad, can I have some money?" You're liable to get a big fat no. Likewise, if you ask your mom for money when she's scrubbing a toilet, or if you ask your dad when he's cleaning the after dinner dishes, the answer is also likely to be no. It's a game of cat and mouse and you really have to use as much finesse as you can possibly muster.

I figured I would wait until everyone was finished with their dinner and we were getting ready to enjoy a sweet treat for dessert. Here's the genius of my plan: I wouldn't actually use the word 'money'. That would be far too direct. Instead, I would say something about the skateboard. I might bring up how a friend and I were looking at it and how he's going to be getting one. I might talk about all of the things it would allow me to do. How it would make me a better student, and better at hand eye coordination. It would certainly contribute to an increase in my physical fitness, which was important these days, especially with the news always doing stories on how fat we kids are.

Another thing I was thinking about was how to let them know that I would need money, without actually saying that I needed money. I was thinking about saying things like 'too bad I can't afford it', or that it's really not that 'expensive'. Things like that, that definitely gave a strong hint as to what I was looking for without being too direct.

When I got home, mom already had dinner on the table and my father was just getting home from work. I ran to the bathroom and washed up. I spent a few extra minutes looking in the mirror to make sure that I had just the right mixture of cute and pouty. I've found over the years that it's about 20% what you say and 80% how you look and sound while you're saying it. Those figures seem to be slightly skewed from previous years. It used to be 5% what you said and 95% how you looked and sounded. But, as we all know, as you grow up it becomes easier to say no to us. That's just a fact of life. I'm pretty sure my parents have gotten to the point where people have no problem saying no to them.

I pulled my chair out from the table and sat down, ready to launch my attack. And then I started to notice that something was terribly wrong. There was no steam coming off my broccoli or potatoes. I glanced in my mother's direction, making sure I didn't make eye contact. Her lips were pursed and her eyes were more wrinkly than usual, especially along the sides. She was glaring off into space. I quickly brought my own gaze down toward my lap and noticed that the tablecloth was bobbing up and down where my mother's foot would've been.

This was not good. Cold dinner, angry mother.

My father sidled up to the table and dropped hard into his chair. He turn red toward my mother and they shared a look that said I was in trouble. My father scratched his head and looked down at his plate. "Where were you this afternoon, Jake?"

I rolled a broccoli floret around with my fork and then started playing with my mashed potatoes. It was the dinner table version of kicking your feet in the dirt while you're trying to come up with an answer for something that there was no good answer for. In the end, I remained silent, hoping that this line of questioning would eventually pass.

My father was not so willing to give up, however. "Were you at Berkman's again?"

"Yes," I said. "But I can explain."

My father put his hand up to stop me from going into some long, drawn out story about why I was there and why I thought it wouldn't be a big deal. "We've had this discussion before. You are to come straight home after school, unless you have permission from your mother or me. Did you have permission?"

"No," I surrendered. I put my fork down gently on the edge of my plate. The metallic sound it made rang out loudly through the silent curtain of awkward tension that had been draped across our dinner.

"What are you looking at while you're there?" My mother asked. "You were there for hours today and you didn't come home with a single thing."

"It's nothing," I answered pitifully. There was no need to bring up what I'd been doing. It was pointless. There was no way I was going to be able to convince them to get it for me now.

My mother's voice softened. "It's hard to believe that nothing would make you as late for supper as you were."

"It's called the *Street Shredder*," I muttered.

My mother gave my father a quick look across the table. It wasn't exactly what I would call a look to get hopeful about. But it wasn't quite the dismissive look I'd been expecting.

THE CARD

I settled into bed that night with *The Toothpaste Millionaire*, a book my English Teacher had suggested for me the week before. I was looking for something a little different from the norm. I love reading about dragons and witches and wizards as much as the next kid, but sometimes it gets to be somewhat redundant. The stories, though I love them, can be a bit stale and monotonous if you read more then three of them in a row. It's like when you eat that first piece of pizza and it tastes so good. Then you go back for a second piece and a third piece and they also taste wonderful. But eventually, you get to fourth or fifth...or for some kids, the sixth, and that pizza doesn't taste so great on account of you've had your fill.

Your stomach starts to rumble and saltiness of the crust and cheese starts to rub the sensation from your taste buds.

There was a knock on my door as I was finishing up my thirty minutes of reading for the night. My father peeked in and said, "Can we talk?"

"Sure," I answered, putting my bookmark in my book and setting it on my bedside table.

He came over and sat on the edge of my bed. "I wanted to talk to you about something you mentioned at dinner." I sat up a little taller, propping myself up against the wall. "You said something about a skateboard you were looking at at Berkman's."

I wasn't quite sure what to say. It seemed like this was going in a positive direction and I didn't want to do anything to jeopardize it. "Yes," I replied. "It's called the *Street Shredder*." I was very careful not to talk about the fact that I couldn't afford it and I needed money. I wanted to see where he was going to take this.

"How much does it cost?" He asked. That didn't take long, I thought to myself. I figured I would have to finesse my way into that, but he just put it right out there in the open.

Before we go any farther, I should tell you that my father is a businessman. It's his job to talk to people about money and prices of things.

"It's a lot," I said.

"How much is a lot?" He asked, "Don't beat around the bush, just tell me."

"It's like a hundred dollars, or something crazy like that," I said. I should've known better than to be so vague. I was trying my own negotiating strategy. And it might have worked if I was talking to one of my friends. But my dad has a little more experience than that.

"What's 'like' a hundred dollars? Does that mean it's one hundred dollars exactly? Or does it mean it's a little more or a little less?" His gaze was intense. I knew he was in my bedroom, getting ready to say goodnight, but it seemed like he was smack dab in the middle of one of his work meetings.

"It's One Hundred and four dollars and ninety eight cents," I said, finally coming clean.

He stood up and walked across the room toward the door. He quickly peeked his head out into the hallway. Satisfied with whatever he saw or didn't see, he shut the door and walked back over to my bed.

"That's a lot of money for a skateboard. Are you sure you want it?"

I could feel the hope inside of me rising. Was it really going to be this easy? The next day at this time I'd be the proud owner of the *Street Shredder*, going to bed and dreaming about all of the amazing, death defying tricks I'd be able to do. I felt my head start to nod uncontrollably. I must've looked like a twelve year old bobble head doll. "Yes,"

I blurted out, "I want it more than anything!"

He stroked his chin with his left hand. I'd seen this look before. He was pretending to think about whether or not he wanted to give me that much money. Every time I really wanted something he put me through this little charade. "You're getting older, Jake."

Uh oh. He'd never said this before. What was this all about? What did it matter how old I was? If nothing else, the fact that I was getting older would work in my favor in getting something as potentially dangerous as a skateboard.

"I've been thinking an awful lot lately about how I'm going to teach you about the value of money and responsibility."

Value? Resposibility? I was starting to wish he'd never come into my room. I'd have been better off if he'd just popped his head in the door and said 'goodnight' and kept walking to his room. But he hadn't done that. And now I was sitting on my bed with nowhere to run and nowhere to hide, an impending conversation about value and responsibility preparing to slap me in the face.

My father continued. "You know son, money isn't something that's just given to you. As you get older, you're going to find that you actually have to work quite hard for it. And because you have to work so hard to get it, you become considerably more thoughtful about what you choose to buy with it. Do you understand?"

I nodded.   I was speechless…and disappointed.   He was telling me that I wasn't getting the skateboard and that life is hard and blah blah blah.   I just wanted to fast forward to bedtime.

"I'm hoping you'll understand why I've decided not to give you the money for the skateboard. I'm also hoping that you take what I do give you and use it in a way that will allow you to get far more than just that skateboard."

Just a skateboard?   Just a skateboard? What was he talking about?   It wasn't just a skateboard.   There was no way he could give me anything that could be worth more to me than the *Street Shredder*.

He reached his hand into the pocket of his shirt. The motion was smooth and refined, developed over many years of business meetings. What he held in his hand was less than impressive. My father continued to hold it directly under my nose, waiting for me to take hold of it. But I couldn't bring myself to take it.

"Alright," He said, "Suit yourself." He set it on top of my book and walked to the door. His hand rested on the knob and before he turned it he said, "It's yours to keep. I know you're upset, but give it some thought. If you get your head in the right place, you could use that to do a lot of things."

After he'd gone, I took one last look at it and turned off the light. I settled into bed and tried to get to sleep. But I couldn't sleep. I just kept thinking: How am I supposed to get over a hundred dollars with just some stupid old baseball card.

THE SPARK

I hardly spoke to either of my parents the next day at breakfast. I kept my head down and muddled through my cereal and orange juice. When I was finished I threw on my backpack and practically ran out the door.

"You look thrilled to be alive!" My friend TJ was waiting out in front of my house. He was dressed in all green. TJ was something of an anomaly. He was what the kids at school liked to call 'fashionably challenged,' which would normally mean he got picked on and treated like an outcast. But in TJ's case, the kids made a major exception. I think this was mostly because TJ was hands down the funniest kid anyone knew. In fact, I'm pretty sure they thought that his mismatched get ups were part of his comedy routine. I knew differently, and so did TJ.   You see, TJ is the result of what happens when your mother starts letting you pick out your own clothes at age two and then never tells you that you can't wear the ridiculous outfit you picked out.   Today's clothing collage consisted of a neon green pair of sweat pants with the word 'win' written in bold black letters on both legs, a baseball cap that was such a dark shade of green it was almost black, and the center piece of the whole ensemble, a shirt that had nothing on it, except the face of Oscar the Grouch.

"Yeah," I shot back, "well you look like a train wreck."

"I know," he said taking a big whiff of fresh air.   "There's something about it that just seems so liberating!"   He walked for a few more steps with his chest puffed out and then came back down to Earth. "So, what's wrong?"

"N o t h i n g , " I a n s w e r e d . "Something…everything."

"I think I might have a cure for that," he smiled. "Seriously, though, if you could narrow it down, I might actually be able to help you."

I told him about dinner the night before and then about the awkward talk with my dad afterward. I pulled the baseball card from my jean pocket. "I think he expects me to use this to get the skateboard."

"You know what," TJ said, "I think from now on we better keep your problems as broad as possible." We walked for a block and a half and then

TJ stopped in his tracks. "Let me see that card again." I handed him the card and he examined it thoroughly, flipping it back and forth. He held it up close to his face and then pushed it out away from his face. He examined the edges before turning his eyes to the corners.

"Do you really see something, or is this just some kind of joke?"

He held up a finger and shushed me. "Things like this take time, Jake. Let the master do his work." I watched closely as his eyes scanned back and forth from one end of the card to the other. And then he flipped the card over and did the same examination on the back. "I've come to a conclusion," he said when he was done.

"And..."

"At first glance, it would appear as though your father has given you a lot of extra work.   And he has, there's no doubt about that.   However, he has set you up for success."

"What do you mean?" I asked.

"Take a look at this card," he said, holding the card out in front of me. I'd been so angry the night before that I hadn't really taken the time to look at the card clearly.   "Do you see the corners?" TJ continued. I nodded that I did.   "Notice how sharp they are. Most kids carry around baseball cards like this and the corners are all rounded and bent. Your father took good care of this, that's why it's in this plastic case."   He gave the card a little flick with his finger to illustrate his point. "Furthermore, this card is over forty years old.   And the player on the card is a hall of famer. Are you putting it together yet?"

"I think so. My father gave me an amazing baseball card and it's supposed to take the place of the skateboard that I really wanted." I was being sarcastic because, to be perfectly honest with you, I was a little bit lost and I had no idea what TJ was getting at.

"Jake," he said, taking my shoulders in his hands, "this card is worth money. Probably not enough to get you the skateboard, but definitely enough to get a good start."

I thought for a moment. Was I supposed to sell this card and then ask my parents to give me the rest of the money for the skateboard? The way my father had spoken to me about the value of money and responsibility I didn't think that sounded like what he was trying to get me to do.

We were just about to school when it hit me. "I know what I'm supposed to do!"

"It's about time," said TJ as though he'd expected me to have this revelation earlier. "Whatcha got?"

"I'm going to sell this card to someone at school. And then I'm going to take that money and go down to that used baseball card shop downtown. I'll use the money to buy more baseball cards and then I'll sell those for more money than I paid for them. Eventually, I'll have enough money to buy the skateboard. I think that's what my father was trying to get me to think of. He's in business. I've heard him talk about selling something and then taking that money and buying more things to sell. I'm pretty sure this is what he meant!"

"You have come far, my child," TJ mocked. "You make your father very proud."

We headed into school ready to take action and make some money.

THE LESSON

"But he's a hall of famer!" I said to the fifth person who had turned me down this morning. As they walked away, I turned to TJ and said, "Selling stuff is a lot harder than I thought it would be."

"Maybe if you didn't start out every sales pitch by saying 'Hey, wanna help me buy a skateboard?' people might be more interested."

"What are you talking about? I'm just trying to be honest with them. I want them to know what they are doing when they buy this card. They would be helping me buy a skateboard. You don't think that would give them some satisfaction?"

"What does your father do again?" TJ asked.

I knew he knew the answer, but I humored him anyway. "Businessman." I knew that if I went along with his line of questioning I would get the worm at the end of it.

"And you're this bad at selling something as easy to sell as this mint condition baseball card."

"You think you could do it better? You think you'd have had it sold by now?"

"Maybe," he said. "Maybe not. But I can guarantee you that I'd have more people interested by now."

"How?"

"First of all, tell me about the last two people you just tried to sell the card to."

I had to think for a minute. I rolled my eyes back into my head and stared up at the ceiling. "I think one of them was..."

"See, right there,' TJ said. "You don't even know who you were talking to. If you're going to sell something to someone, you have to be observant. You have to pick up on their subtleties. Look at their eyes - are they looking at you or away from you? Are they looking at the card in your hand, or at their watch?"

I nodded. That made good sense. I had no idea TJ was a ninja salesman.

"The next thing you need to do is target the right type of people for the product you're selling. No offense, but three of the first five people you've tried to sell that card to were girls on the cheerleading team. They were wearing their uniforms for crying out loud."

"So."

"Cheerleaders don't cheerlead because they enjoy watching sports. They cheerlead because it's time to hang out with other girls and do something fun. They cheerlead because it's time they get to spend staring at a boy they like. But if you go up to a cheerleader after the game and ask them who won, they probably won't be able to tell you. And if they are able to tell you, they'll probably tell you the score with the lowest number first. Do you remember who the other two people that you tried to sell to were?"

"Not really," I said, my palms starting to get sweaty. I felt like I was under attack by my best friend. Where did he learn all of this stuff. I never knew TJ was so smart.

"They were nerds. Now, nerds are cool, but most of them are not really into baseball. They like video games and computer programming. They're into Star Wars and Minecraft - not collecting baseball cards."

"So who do you suggest I 'target'?" I asked sharply.

TJ looked around. We were in the hallway before class was set to begin, so there was no shortage of people. He pointed over to a group of people huddled around the drinking fountain. "Which one of those four people would you approach with your card."

I looked them over. There was a girl in a cheerleader outfit, a boy in a Lord of the Rings shirt, another girl in jeans and a pink sweater and a boy in a football jersey. "I would say out of those four, I might pick the kid in the jersey."

"Now you're getting it," he said.

"But it's not a baseball uniform. It's a football jersey."

"That's correct, however, most kids who like football will also like baseball, basketball and hockey. There are exceptions, but most sports lovers love most sports."

I started to walk over to the boy in the jersey when I felt TJ's hand on my shoulder pulling me back. "Not so fast," he said.

"What?"   I was becoming annoyed. "You just told me I picked the right person. What more is there?"

"Based on they way you were talking to the first five people, there's quite a bit. It's time for lesson two.   The most important thing in selling, once you've got the right audience, is to make everything about the potential buyer."

"What's that mean?"

"What that means is that instead of talking about what buying this card is going to do for you, you have to let them know what buying the card is going to do for them. They need to see a value in what they are getting, otherwise they're going to look at you like a charity. And no kid's going to part with their lunch money for a charity."

This made sense, but I didn't know how. "How am I supposed to make it about them? What do I do?"

"The first thing you need to do is find out how much that card is worth. That'll give you some good information and it will add to value of your offer to them."

I was confused again. "What do you mean my offer to them? Wouldn't I just sell it to them for what it's worth?"

"You could do that if you owned your own shop and they came in looking for that card specifically. But in your situation, you are the one trying to make the sale. So, you're going to make it a point to tell them what the card's worth and then you're going to sell it for far less than that. This will make them feel like they're getting a great deal."

"But if I sell it for far less than it's worth I won't be making money on it, will I?"

TJ the pointed out the obvious. "How much did you pay for it in the first place?"

"Nothing, my dad gave it to me."

"Exactly," he said. "So any money you make on it is a profit that you can take and use to buy more things to sell."

"I see your point," I said. "So, how do we find the value of the card?"

TJ smiled and said, "I'll show you."

THE PRICE

We ducked into the computer lab before class began and logged onto a computer in the far corner. Waiting for the computer to boot up, I began thinking about *The Toothpaste Millionaire*. A boy named Rufus was able to make a million dollars selling toothpaste very cheaply. I looked down at the baseball card in my hand and wondered if I could ever make a million dollars selling baseball cards?

"Do you have the card?" TJ asked as he loaded up the internet. "I hate the school's internet. It's always so slow."

Giving him the card, I pulled up a chair next to him. "So, how do we do this?"

"It's quite simple really. We just have to do a Google search for the value of the card we have. We'll need to know the player, card manufacturer and year. This information is all printed on the card in one place or another."

"That's it?"

"That's it," he said. He looked at the card, studying it again. "I can't believe your father gave you this. Are you sure he would want you to sell it?"

That was an interesting question. I hadn't given it that much thought. I just assumed that he was trying to tell me to do something with it. I was pretty sure he was giving it to me to sell. That seemed like the only really logical reason to give it to me. Otherwise, he had given me the worst possible substitution gift.

"I'm pretty sure that's why he gave it to me," I said after a minute.

The Google page had loaded and TJ began typing frantically. This kid was amazing. He set the card down on the computer console and typed the name 'Henry Aaron'. He hit enter and bingo, we were staring at the very card that was sitting in front of us.

My jaw dropped. "It's worth that much money?"

"I guess so," TJ said staring at the screen.

I picked up the card and examined it more closely than I had before. I couldn't believe that this rectangular piece of cardboard with a picture on the front and some statistics on the back could be worth so much money. It wouldn't be enough to get me the *Street Shredder*, but it would be a good start.

I was starting to feel good about things and then TJ finally averted his gaze from the screen. "I don't think this is necessarily a good thing," he said.

"What do you mean? This card's worth $70. How could that not be a good thing?"

"Let's consider our earlier sales strategy. We were going to find out the value of the card and then sell it for slightly less, giving the buyer a deal." He paused here, allowing me time to process. "Well, let's say we want to give the buyer a 30% reduction in cost. We'd be selling this particular card for $50."

"That's great!" I said, "I don't see a problem with that."

And then TJ hit me with the reality of the situation. "Who are you going to find in this school that brings $50 for lunch money?"

I thought for a few minutes and couldn't think of a single person who would have more than $5 in their backpacks. "Great," I finally said. "My dad gives me this great card to sell and I can't find anyone who has enough money to buy it. It might as well be useless. What if I just sold it to someone for a couple of dollars?"

"You're not very bright sometimes," TJ said. He swiveled in his chair and brought his hands up, ready to gesture. He was serious now. "Look, you have something fairly valuable here. You don't want to go and sell it as cheaply as you can just so you can be rid of it. If the buyers aren't here, we have to go find them."

"What do you suggest?"

"Meet me after school," TJ said with a grin, "I'll get you to the right place."

THE SALE

I met TJ out in front of the school when the day was over. The memories of last night's dinner were buzzing around in my head. "TJ," I said, "we have to stop at my house before we go anywhere."

"Why?" he asked.

"Because," I said, "Last night I spent a few hours after school over at Berkman's. I didn't tell my mom about it and she was pretty upset when I got home."

He nodded, "We have to hurry then. The place we're going closes at five."

My mother didn't offer any resistance to the idea of me going somewhere with

TJ. She was just happy that I stopped and asked. Plus, for some reason, both of my parents really like TJ. He has this kind of indescribable charm about him that grown ups go gaga for. My mom just said that I needed to be home by five thirty for supper.

We were off, rushing down the street in the direction of the business section of town. "So, where are we going?" I huffed.

"Beckett's Cards and More," TJ said between breaths. "Hold on a second." He stopped and pulled an inhaler out of his pocket. He pushed the top and sucked in a large gulp of medicated air. "We're going to have to slow down." He looked at his watch. "It's almost 4:30. We'll make it."

Walking slightly slower than before, TJ's breathing started to regulate itself. Once I was sure that he would be okay, I asked him, "So, what do we do at Beckett's Cards and More?"

"There's a guy who works there. He specializes in this sort of thing. We'll bring the card to him and tell him what we want for it and then he'll tell us what he's willing to give us. We'll work our way down from our original price and he'll come up from his. It's called bargaining...and I know how to bargain. I'll get you more for that card than you would've gotten. It won't be $70 dollars, but it'll be more than some kid's lunch money."

"So what's my job in this whole thing?"

"You're supplying the card. Just leave the rest to me. And whatever you do, don't say a word."

"Okay," I nodded.

We arrived at Beckett's at about twenty minutes of five. TJ assured me that was more than enough time to get a deal done and have money in my pocket before dinner.

Beckett's was a place that I'd walked past many times in my life but never noticed. It was quite unremarkable. The storefront was narrow and since it was located between the town pharmacy and the arcade, it was easy to miss. TJ opened the door and a 'ding dong' chime came on. As we passed through the threshold we heard a buzzing sound as each of our legs passed a concealed plastic frog. We walked up a ramp that led us through a dark hallway with lots of papers posted to the wall. These were advertisements for dog walkers, baby sitters, local bands.

When we got to the top of the ramp, the store opened up a bit. It was still pretty narrow, but at least I could put my arms out without feeling like I'd take down someone's sale's pitch. There were posters of baseball players, football players, basketball players, and soccer players all over the walls, and even some hung on the ceiling. Two long glass cases ran the length of the shop. Inside the cases were thousands of cards from players of every sport you could imagine. The lights on the ceiling kept the shop dim, but the lights inside these cases were bright to show off the merchandise.

As we approached the section of the case that had a cash register on it, a man approached us. He was a thin man, not much taller than we were. He was wearing a Derek Jeter T-shirt, glasses hanging from the collar.

"Can I help you boys?" he asked. He didn't look at me, but gave TJ a slow and awkward inspection. "Nice outfit," he smirked.

"Thanks," TJ said, his face beaming with pride.

"That's not a compliment kid."

TJ stayed calm and ignored the man's insults. He looked at me and I handed him the card. He put the card down on the counter and said, "How much will you give us for this?"

The man took a flashlight from the back pocket of his jeans and clicked it on. He shined it on the face of the card. "Got yourself a Hank Aaron card, eh?" He moved his fingers toward the card and then lifted his eyes toward us. "May I?" he asked. TJ nodded and the man gently picked the card up and examined it, much the same way TJ had earlier in the day. He looked at everything. It took him several minutes and at one point he even brought out a small magnifying glass. "Alright boys, here's the deal. You've got a really nice card here. It's in great shape and you really couldn't ask for a better ball player. The problem is, this particular version of the card is not really sought out by collectors. Some Hank Aaron cards go for thousands of dollars. I can't give you that for this one. What I can do is probably closer to twenty five."

TJ picked the card up off the counter and slid it into the pocket of his sweatpants.   "You sir, ought to be ashamed of yourself, trying to low ball a couple of kids. Twenty five dollars might sound like a lot of money to most of the *children* that come into this shop, but not us.   We know how much this card's worth and I know that when we leave you're going to turn around and sell it for at least seventy five dollars, if not more.   So, I'm going to give you one more chance to give us a fair offer, or we're going to take your future profits and go."

I couldn't believe what I was hearing come from TJ's mouth. Was this the kid that I'd grown up with who could barely dress himself and only seemed to care about video games? I had to look at his green sweatpants and Oscar the Grouch shirt to remind myself that this was, in fact, my friend.   I was beginning to wonder what else I didn't know about TJ.

The man folded his arms across his chest and brought one hand up to his chin. He rubbed the sides of his jaws with his thumb and index finger and stared at TJ with a raised eyebrow. "Well, I'm not going to give you seventy five dollars, that's for sure. I have to make some sort of profit on this deal."

"I'm not expecting an offer of seventy five dollars. I know how things work. But I was certainly expecting something a little less insulting," TJ said, standing his ground.

"I'll give you forty," The man offered.

"Sixty," TJ countered.

"Forty five, not a cent more."

"Fifty five," TJ said, "not a cent less."

"Forty six."

"Fifty five."

The man pursed his lips and began sucking air in through his teeth. "Let me see the card again." TJ pulled the card back out and set it on the counter. The man picked it up and gave it another look. "I'll go as high as fifty, but that's it, absolutely my final offer."

"Deal!" TJ said, reaching out his hand. The man shook it and gave TJ fifty dollars from the register and then began filling out some information in a book.

We emerged from the store victorious. My friend TJ had gotten me fifty dollars for the card. I gave him ten for all the help he gave me. I couldn't wait to get home and tell my father about the money and how TJ had bargained with the card shop man. But then TJ brought me back down to Earth.

"You know," he said. "That's not enough to get that skateboard. From where I'm standing, your real work is just beginning."

THE BUSINESS

That night at dinner I decided not to tell my parents about the money from the card. I could tell that my father had wanted to ask about it, but didn't want to force the issue.

When I went to bed, instead of reading, I sat and thought about how I could turn forty dollars into a hundred dollars. It would stand to reason that I could buy more baseball cards and sell those. The problem was, with forty dollars, I doubted I could get anything with real value that the kids would be into. And then it clicked in my head, like a switch.

I had seen them on the counter at Beckett's. There were packs of Yugogi cards for sale for three dollars per pack. The kids at school were really into these. The kids would trade cards with each other and talk about the power level of each character card. The cards with the most power had the most value.

I also knew a number of kids who didn't have cards because their parents wouldn't take them downtown to Beckett's or give them any money to buy such things.

I did some figuring. A pack of Yugogi cards ran three dollars. Each pack included fifteen cards. Every set of fifteen cards contained three power cards and twelve cards of lesser value. The value of these last twelve cards varied.

I would sell each of the power cards for three dollars, just a little more than the cost of a school lunch. That would give me my money back times three! I could then bargain and haggle with kids over the cost of the last twelve cards. I would accept anywhere from fifty cents to two dollars per card for these last twelve. Even if I was only able to get fifty cents for the last twelve cards, that would still be six dollars. Plus the nine that I would make from the three power cards, that would bring my total to fifteen dollars per pack. At fifteen dollars per pack, to get to a hundred dollars, I'd have to sell seven packs.

Twenty one dollars. That would be my cost to get started. I went to bed very satisfied with myself. I couldn't wait for school to be over the next day so I could go over to Beckett's and buy seven packs of Yugogi cards!

THE GAME

"What's the problem, kid?"

The man at Beckett's was standing behind the register looking down at me, expecting me to hand him twenty one dollars for the seven packs of Yugogi cards I'd just placed down on the counter.

"What's the problem Jake?" TJ asked. "Give him the money."

I fumbled a bit, but eventually pulled two twenty dollar bills from my jean pockets. I handed them over to the man and watched as he threw them in register and counted out a ten, a five and four ones and tossed them on the counter in front of me. I gathered the money while the man put the cards in a small plastic grocery bag.

"Have a nice day," he said with a smile that looked less than sincere.

"Thanks, you too," TJ said, filling the awkward silence.

When were outside the store and walking back home, TJ asked, "What was that all about? That wasn't the kid who told me all about this amazing business plan in school today."

"I know," I said. "It's just, I'm having second thoughts."

"Why? Your plan's rock solid."

"I guess I'm just feeling like, I don't know, maybe I'm ripping kids off by selling these cards for more than they could buy an entire pack."

TJ stopped. "Are you serious?"

"Yeah," I said, "I guess I am."

"Let me help put this into perspective for you. The kids you're planning on selling to, would they be able to play Yugogi without you selling them cards? Do they have any other way of getting these cards? No. Because their parent won't take them to the store to buy them. You are putting your own time and effort into going to the store to get the cards and giving them access to something they desperately want. It's called supply and demand. You have the supply - and since they can't get them anywhere else, the cards you have will be in demand. I, personally, think you could probably charge more than you're charging."

"Yeah, you said that earlier," I reminded him. "I don't know, it just feels wrong."

"Well, you could just charge less than you were planning on. You might want to bring the cost of a power card down to two dollars instead of three and keep all the other cards at a quarter. You'd still make money, it'll just take you longer to get to your goal."

We walked for a little while and when we were almost to my house TJ chimed in again.

"Just in case you wanted something else to think about. Do you know what the going rate is for a power card?"

"What do you mean the going rate?"

"You do know that the kids who have these cards sell them too, right? They don't just trade with other cardholders. They try to make it worth their while, financially speaking, so they can go get more cards."

I looked down at the cards I'd just bought, feeling like such an idiot for just jumping into this without seeing what other people were doing. "If other people are selling these, there's no need for me to start selling these. I just waisted half of the money!"

TJ was shaking his head. "Are you sure your dad's a business man? You must not listen to him at all." He paused for a second, giving me time to come to my senses before he continued. "The going rate for a power card as of two

O'clock this afternoon was ten dollars. Now, that has been up and down the last couple weeks. Some days you can luck out and get one for seven, but most days it hangs around the ten, or even twelve dollar range."

"So, you're saying I should sell the cards at a higher price than I was thinking?" I didn't want to do this. I was already feeling guilty about charging them the pack price for one card.

"No," TJ said. A maniacal look came across his face, a deep smile leading the way. "I'm saying you become the hero for the little guys. You are the business with principles. You are going to be the guy who doesn't take advantage of their deepest desire to play with the big boys. Sell your cards at the price you were originally thinking and people will flock

to you! You'll go through all seven packs
by lunch tomorrow, guaranteed!"

THE AFTERMATH

TJ and I sat down for lunch. It had been a whirlwind morning. TJ went around as soon as we arrived at school, drumming up business in the hallway. Actually, he just stood in the middle of the hallway and shouted, "Jake has a great deal on Yugogi cards! Best deal in the school! Get them while supplies last!"

That was all it took. I had cards separated by power cards and basic cards. The power cards went in a matter of minutes. It was border line chaos as kids lined up, some pushing and shoving to get the best cards they could for their money. What surprised me was how quickly the fifty cent cards were sold. Most kids bought ten or twelve of them. I would learn later that the kids would trade as many as five or six of these cards for a power card.

By the time the first bell rang, signaling classes were to commence, I was left standing in the hallway with a stack of money in one hand and an empty grocery bag in the other. I thought to myself that this might be the beginning of something very cool. I headed for my locker to get my books for class, quite satisfied with everything.

"So what are you going to do now?" TJ asked between bites of his popcorn chicken.

"What do you mean what am I going to do now?" I asked.

"Well, you made roughly a hundred and five dollars this morning. Plus you have another nineteen at home. That's gotta be enough to buy that skateboard."

"Yeah," I said. He was right, but my interests had shifted slightly. The skateboard would be there. And I knew that I had enough to pick it up anytime I wanted. "I'll tuck some of that money aside, but I think I'm going to go back to Beckett's tonight."

"Why? Wasn't the point of everything to make enough money to get the *Street Shredder*?"

"It was at first. But we're onto something here." I handed him thirty dollars. "This is my way of saying thanks for getting me started on this little adventure."

"Gee thanks!" he said, his eyes beaming. "I was just helping out, I didn't expect any money. Are you sure?"

"I'm sure. I know I can do this again tomorrow and make at least double what I made today. Like I said, I'll get the skateboard, but there's also one other thing I need to get."

"What's that?" he asked.

"You'll see," I said with a sly grin.

THE STREET SHREDDER

After school I zipped down to Beckett's and bought another ten packs of cards. The total came to just over thirty dollars. This left me with forty-five dollars, plus the nineteen at home. I wanted to make sure I had some money left over, just in case these sets of cards didn't sell as fast as this morning's sets. If they did sell as fast, I would have two hundred and fourteen dollars.

I was cautious about things, and as it turned out, I had reason to be. The next day, I sold all of the cards and ended up with the hundred and fifty dollars I had set out to earn. However, it took me nearly all day to move the cards. The day before, I'd been mobbed by all of the kids who wanted a seat at the Yugogi table. Today, there were still quite a few kids who either didn't have the money the day before, or didn't get to me before I sold out of cards. However, the mob was much smaller. I sold about half the cards first thing, which was still seventy five dollars, but nowhere near what I had intended to do.

"What do I do now?" I asked TJ as we walked to class.

"Well so far, you've learned about supply and demand. When there's a demand and you have the supply, it's easy to sell. Now you need to learn about the hustle." He smiled a little as he said this. I had to admit, I was smiling too, but for a far different reason. His yellow corduroy pants were rubbing and it sounded very similar to a fart. And the smile on his face was just devious enough to look like he knew it.

"What's the hustle?" I asked, barely getting the words out through my laughter.

"The hustle is the work. You are now going to have to put forth more effort to sell these cards. You'll have to find people who are interested in Yugogi and convince them to buy your cards. Up till now, people have just been fawning over your cards, but not anymore."

I was afraid of this. It had seemed too good to be true, but I couldn't help but get sucked into the idea that all I had to do was get these cards and people would just flock to me and give me their money. Now, I was about to see what kind of a salesman I could be.

As it turned out, I was much better at selling Yugogi cards than I had been just a few days earlier with my father's baseball card.   I think it might have something to do with the fact that kids aren't really into baseball cards the way they were when my dad was a kid.

By three O'clock all of the cards were gone, but I was left wondering what I was going to do the next day. If today made one thing clear to me, it was that people were not going to buy more Yugogi cards from me the next day.

"Yeah," TJ agreed as we were walking home. "You saturated the market."

"Saturated the market? What's that?"

"You really don't talk to your dad much do you?" He smirked and stopped in the middle of the sidewalk. "Jake, think about a sponge. You take it and slowly dip it into a tub of water and it soaks up the water for a time. The kids you were selling to the other day were your market, the sponge. The cards you were selling was the —"

"Water!" I interrupted, excited that I was understanding where he was going with this. "And the more water you put into the sponge, the less it will accept. The rest of the water stays in the tub. Just like, the more cards I put into the market, the less it can accept. And the cards, instead of staying in a tub, stay in my bag!"

"Very good," TJ nodded. "I'm impressed."

"So now I've got to find another sponge."

"If you want to keep selling things to people, you're going to have to. Of course, you could just take your money and go buy that skateboard and be done with it."

He had a point. We walked quickly over to Berkman's. I had more than enough money in my pocket from the day. I walked to the back of the store and found a clerk. He was nice enough to get *The Street Shredder* down.

I took the board in my hand and admired the artwork on the back. The dragon was fierce, the red background merging perfectly with its scaly green body. I ran my finger along the belly of the beast and was amazed at how smooth it was. I took the most perfect thing I'd ever held by the front wheels and brought it to the front of the store.

"That's sweet," TJ said after we'd left the store. "You're going to let me have a ride on it right?" He nudged me and winked.

"Sure," I said, "but not until I break her in. And not until you get a helmet." I gave him a little nudge and wink of my own.

THE PAYBACK

TJ showed up at my house the next day wearing a helmet. "I'm ready to ride your new skateboard to school, Master Jake." He bowed as he said this.

I had to laugh. "There's no way you're riding my skateboard wearing those pink pants. Or that Elmo sweatshirt."

He stood up from his bow. "What's wrong with these? They're great."

"Sure," I said. "They're great. Just not for riding *The Street Shredder*." I put my helmet on and stepped onto the board. "Don't worry, I'll go slow enough for you to keep up."

***

After school I rode over to Beckett's while TJ walked. I had one last thing to do before I could fully enjoy my skateboard.

I walked up the dark and narrow ramp and over to the counter. I began scanning the selection. I didn't see it right away, but by the time the man running the shop came over I had spotted it. "I would like to buy that one," I said.

The man looked at me curiously. "Do you want to negotiate or are you fine paying sticker price?"

"Sticker price is fine."

TJ was over by the Yugogi cards and said, "Hey, check these out!"

I went over and saw a cardboard display that was easily double the size of the Yugogi display. It read 'Niyaki - The New Game That's Sweeping the Nation'. I took one of the packages in my hand and read about how it was based on an ancient Japanese ritual that has now started to spread world wide. I looked up at TJ. "You thinking what I'm thinking?"

"Absolutely," he said.

I turned to the man behind the counter. "How much are these?"

"Five per pack," He shot back.

"I'll take three packs," I said. I turned to TJ, "Let's see if we can move them before we make a major investment. If they sell, we'll be in good shape. I haven't seen any of these at school. We'll be on the cutting edge!"

He pretended to start crying and leaned on me. "You have come so far in such a short time!"

***

That night before bed, my father came into my room. He had just gotten home from work. He said he had a long day and a late meeting and that he was sorry for missing dinner. He looked over toward my closet and saw *The Street Shredder* propped up against the door.

"M o m   s a i d   y o u   g o t   t h a t . Congratulations," he said, a proud smile on his face.

"Yeah," I said.   "Well, I couldn't have done it without you."

"What do you mean?" He asked. "You must've done something right on your own.   There's no way that card was enough."

"No," I said.   "It wasn't.   But it was the right lesson at the right time."

He got up and started to leave.

"Dad, wait," I said, reaching for my nightstand drawer.   I opened it and pulled out a thin brown bag.   "I got something for you."

He stopped and looked at me quizzically. I handed him the bag and he slowly pulled out the Hank Aaron card that he'd given me a few days earlier. I can't be sure, but I'm pretty confident that I saw his eyes tear up a little. He didn't say a word, just looked me in the eyes, nodded his head and left my room looking at his 'new' card.

Books By Justin Johnson

Coby Collins
Coby Collins and the Hex Bolt of Doom
Coby Collins and the Diary of Tingledowner
Coby Collins and the Tunnels of Marley
Coby Collins and the Battle at Bale
The Complete Coby Collins

Zack and Zebo (6 Books)
Zack and Zebo: The Complete Series

Scab and Beads: Locket's Away
Scab and Beads: Milk Mayhem
Scab and Beads: Homework Heist

The Card

Short Stories
A Kid in King William's Court
Sarah and the Search for the Pot of Gold
The Dance Recital
The Kick
Farty Marty
Flick!
Skeeter Skunk and the Glandular Funk
Run Away Bones
Do Not Feed the Zombies
Grade School Super Hero

Collections
Farty Marty: And Other Stories
Do Not Feed the Zombies: And Other Stories

Made in the USA
Middletown, DE
08 December 2016